Reycraft Books
55 Fifth Avenue
New York, NY 10003

Reycraftbooks.com

Reycraft Books is a trade imprint and trademark of Newmark Learning, LLC.

Copyright © 2020 Reycraft Books

Educators and Librarians: Our books may be purchased in bulk for promotional,
educational, or business use. Please contact sales@reycraftbooks.com.

Library of Congress Control Number: 2020908312

ISBN: 978-1-4788-6964-1

Printed in Dongguan, China. 8557/0720/17254

10 9 8 7 6 5 4 3 2 1

First Edition Hardcover published by Reycraft Books

Reycraft Books and Newmark Learning, LLC, support diversity and
the First Amendment, and celebrate the right to read.

Wolf Cub's Song

by
Joseph Bruchac

illustrated by
Carlin Bear Don't Walk

Wolf Cub was sad.
She felt alone and small.
She curled up inside her
den into a furry ball.

"It is so very, very dark.
I can't go play outside.
My friend the Sun who
smiled his light on us
has gone to hide."

"I feel so all
alone,
   alone,
      alone,"
poor Wolf Cub cried.

Just then, Mother Wolf arrived
and looked into the den.

"Do not be sad, my little one.
We're not alone," she said.

"Grandmother Moon and all the stars
are ready to dance up in the sky."

"They're waiting for us to sing,
my little one. Come out and see."

Wolf Cub turned to peek outside.
All the other wolves were waiting there!

"Wolf Cub," they called, "we need your help!"

"The moon and stars up in the sky
wait now for us to come and sing
so they can dance up high."

"We need your voice to sing with us and help complete our song."

"Can I really help you?" Wolf Cub asked.

"You certainly can," all the wolves agreed. "You may be small, but your voice is strong. You're just the singer we all need."

Wolf Cub leapt out of the den and ran outside.

The wolf pack guided her to the hill so high that it touched the sky.

"Are you ready now, my little one?"
her mother asked.

Wolf Cub looked up into the night.
Her heart felt happy and light.

Wolf Cub sang her song.
Then all the other wolves joined in.

"None of us are alone" is what they were singing as Grandmother Moon and all the stars above danced and danced.

Joseph Bruchac

is a writer and traditional storyteller, who lives in the Adirondack Mountains region of northern New York. Much of his work is inspired by his Native American (Abenaki) ancestry. He is the author of more than 130 books for young readers and adults.

Carlin Bear Don't Walk

is an acclaimed Crow and Northern Cheyenne artist from Busby, Montana. His award-winning art is an energetic blend of colorful oils, unique impressionism, and surreal themes. His artwork can be found throughout the world in many galleries, universities, museums, and private collections.